Breath

A Creation Myth Story

Jodi L. Milner

Stone Orchid Press LLC

Breath: A Creation Myth Short Story

Above the crashing sea, high atop the wind-hollowed limestone cliffs, Fauna, the eternal Guardian of Souls, stood at the top of her tower and gazed out over the water. Wind rushed up from the surf and tugged at the fabric of her robe, making it twist and billow out into the open air. She welcomed the breeze with open arms, letting it wash away the tension between her shoulders.

The better part of her day had been spent bent over her worktable sketching the final details of her latest creation, a golden-winged beetle. Bringing the creature to life would have to wait until morning. The hour had grown late, and she had yet to perform her evening communion.

Each life connected to her, like a lacy network of millions of invisible threads stretching over the world. She took a calming breath and extended herself along those lines, seeking out those who needed her guidance and keeping vigil over all that flew, crawled, swam, or slithered. They were her creations, and each evening she became one with them.

In this state of unity, the hours sped by, and when she finished, the sun had already kissed the curved horizon across the great waters. Calls of seabirds echoed from the cliffs and reminded Fauna that she hadn't visited her young friend Apollo in several days.

Apollo, the great albatross, would be out at this hour searching the waves for his dinner. She scouted the silvered clouds for his silhouette and spotted him in the distance, tilting and diving among the rolling swells. He would always be special to her as he was the first and only of all her creations that she had raised.

She had found him when he was a ball of grey fluff that had fallen down the cliff face from his nest among the rocks. He was so adorably helpless that Fauna took him in, feeding and caring for him until he was old enough to hunt on his own.

During his early years, he nested in the safety of the tower's top and often waddled down the narrow stairs to visit her while she worked on her latest designs. Two seasons prior, he finally abandoned the tower to nest with the colony. She couldn't help but miss him, but it was for the best. He needed to be with his own kind.

That evening, Apollo executed his dives and spins with vigor, as if craving a greater thrill riding the wind. It didn't take long to figure out why. High above, a female albatross wheeled in long, slow circles. When he dove, she circled lower. When he spun past her, she turned to follow.

Through the years, Fauna lost count of how many times she had watched the albatross courting ritual. She never tired of it. It was a special delight knowing that Apollo had finally come of age and was ready to select his mate.

The two birds continued their dance as the ocean swallowed the last rays of the sun. Fauna ran down the tower's stairs and through the coarse grass until she reached the rocky cliff face that the albatross colony called home.

As the birds glided past, Fauna extended her hand. Apollo brushed it with the tips of his wing feathers. She opened a mental channel between herself and her friend, letting the tide of his emotions wash through her. It wasn't her habit to pry, but with Apollo, she had a pressing need to be there for him, to let him know of her approval and how pleased she was with him. She refused to miss out on one of the most important moments of his life.

The birds landed and began the elaborate courtship dance. Apollo bobbed and flicked his feathers and warbled a throaty song deep in his chest. The female bowed in acknowledgement and then feigned indifference.

Apollo redoubled his efforts, and Fauna felt his desperation begin to build. She wished there was a way to tell him that it was all an act, that his pairing was secure. The dance progressed and the female began to show her interest, a bob here to match his, an echo of his throaty song there. With each of these cues, Apollo's joy redoubled, and his confidence grew. It wouldn't be long before she accepted him, and they would become a mated pair for life.

A realization sprouted within Fauna, taking root deep in her chest and spreading chills over her body. There, in that intimate moment between the two birds, she had expected to feel their mutual contentment with each other. Instead, she experienced a tenderness so deep and profound that it left her breathless. The sensation was so utterly foreign and thrilling that she had to know more.

She settled her awareness deeper into Apollo's thoughts until she was one with the throbbing of his heart. As he continued the dance, he came alive with an emotion so deep, so vibrant, that her own heart burned with the need to find such a tenderness for herself. With each passing moment, the burn of this need grew more painful until she was forced to pull her awareness away and retreat into the comfort of her tower.

Opposing thoughts swirled inside Fauna's head, and she sought the privacy of her chambers and the comfort of her favorite wicker chair. One moment, she hoped these unexpected new feelings would soon subside and leave her in peace. The next moment, she found herself jealous of what Apollo had. She cursed at herself for not being able to move on. Guardians were supposed to be stronger and more constant than this.

A shriek of wind pulled at her hair and teased the hem of her robe, announcing the arrival of her brother Ventus, the Guardian of Air.

He gusted around the room, rustling bedclothes and tossing papers from the workbench onto the floor, before he settled on the windowsill. The swirl of air slowed and condensed until his pale outline pulled into shape. He reached a transparent hand to her face.

"Why is your face wet?"

His voice reminded her of warm summer breezes. She wiped her eyes with the back of her hand. "They are tears, brother. Have you never cried?"

"Cried? For what reason would I be sad?"

She left the chair and joined him on the window's ledge so she could speak with him face-to-face. "These are not sad tears. To be honest, I'm not quite sure what they are."

He wrinkled his forehead. "Perhaps we can figure it out together. What caused these tears to come?"

"It's not that easy, Ventus." She pulled her knees up under her chin. "I've found something new, and I don't know what it means. It worries me."

"Could you describe it? Our sister Flora has been very creative these days. Maybe it was one of her new flowers?" He slid his hand over hers, his feathery touch like mist on her fingers.

"It wasn't a flower," she answered, annoyed that he would even think that a flower could bring her to tears. "It wasn't a thing at all. It was a feeling. It's like I have been blind to this beautiful emotion that my creations enjoy, and this evening, my eyes were opened." She swallowed and blinked away the tear that threatened to form.

"Well, what was it like?"

Fauna looked out the window, struggling to find the right words to help Ventus understand. "Have you ever wanted to care for someone so much that you would do anything to make them happy?"

He smiled and shrugged his shoulders. "I care for you. I want you to be happy again."

She shook her head. "Imagine that feeling multiplied several hundred times, where your every thought returns to that someone, where you put their needs before yours."

"You're crying again. How is it that talking about it makes you weep?"

"That intense longing to care and be cared for has rooted itself within me. I have been shown that there is something important missing from my life. Now I know about it, I crave it." She placed a hand over her heart. "It hurts in a way I can't describe."

Ventus swayed back and forth, concern pinching his face. "I don't like this. I don't like seeing you this way. I'll speak with Aquata, she's better at figuring out things like this. If she can't help, I will go to Terran. As our eldest brother, he knows more than all of us put together."

Fauna let her head fall back against the stone. "No, don't talk to Terran about this, at least not yet. If this ache doesn't pass, I will go to him myself."

"Are you certain? It would be nothing for me to visit him and return. I could be back within the hour with his advice." Ventus tapped his fingers against his knees. A being made of air wasn't made to be still.

"No, I'm certain. I'd rather speak with him myself. It's been far too long since I've seen him. It would be good for both of us to spend time together."

"Let me know if you change your mind. Until then, I must go. Aquata calls me. She is eager for rain this evening."

"Promise to return?"

"Of course." He turned to gaze out the window into the star filled night. "At the first light of morning, wait for me down on the beach." He bid her farewell and allowed his solid form to dissolve before racing out into the open air and down to where his twin, Aquata, had been waiting for him. The two of them swirled away in a glittering mist that reflected the blue light of the rising moon. Not long after, Fauna heard the low bellows of thunder sounding in the distance.

The night crept by, each second lingering a fraction longer than it should. The hollow ache haunted Fauna and kept her from sleep. Instead, she returned to the window and looked out into the night. Aquata's dark clouds crowded the sky, hiding away the stars and moon, and Ventus had whipped the winds into a frenzy, urging them on faster and faster until the sea below frothed with white caps. The twins always had each other for company. Wind and water, cloud and storm, they were meant to be together and, in a way, completed each other.

Fauna, on the other hand, had walked the earth for centuries, millennia even, and never once had she considered herself alone. And yet she was. There was none other like her in all of creation. Even among her brothers and sisters, only she possessed a beating heart of flesh to enable her to better understand the creatures she governed.

Terran was made from clay and stone and her older sister Flora, from tendril and vine. The twins were made from the water and the air, although they spent most of their time joined as mist and cloud.

Throughout the long night, Fauna reflected on what she had felt between Apollo and his mate. She berated herself for her own stupidity. She should never have allowed herself to be so close during that sensitive time.

Had she kept her distance, she would never have learned how alone she was in the world and could have been spared such anguish. Her existence before had been peaceful, but she felt neither great joy nor sadness. She had been content creating and communing with her creations day in and day out. Now that she knew there was something else, something infinitely more fulfilling, she wanted it.

She wrestled with these thoughts until the first light of dawn made the clouds blush. It was no use pacing and fretting in her bedchamber any longer. She needed the sun on her face and the comforting touch of wind in her hair. She hurried down the glossy foot-worn stairs and plucked her rough woven shawl from its hook to ward off the morning chill.

A narrow path wound its way down the cliff to the white sand beach. Below, a lone sandpiper darted its way in and out of the surf, scolding the water when it dared get too close. Fauna watched the bird dart back and forth and couldn't help but wonder if he too had a mate back at the nest. Did he feel the same powerful urge to care for her as Apollo felt for his mate? She sat in the sand, just out of reach of the bubbling surf and breathed in the fresh salty air as the thoughts from the night before returned in full force.

Down along the beach, Ventus blustered against the sand, kicking small puffs into the air. As he drew closer, he took shape until he walked along the sand. A stream of water extended from the ocean and followed beside him. When Ventus stopped in front of Fauna, the water lifted and spun upward into Aquata's sleek fluid form.

She took a seat alongside Fauna on the sand. "You are still troubled. I can see it. I was hoping that maybe this would fade with sleep. Had I known how much you were hurting, I would have come to you last night. I might have been able to ease your heart."

"What do you know of how I feel?" Fauna asked, digging her toes into the sand. She didn't want to meet her sister's eyes, not yet. It angered her that Aquata assumed she understood. How could she? How could either of them understand? She, like Ventus, had never been alone before. Even at her conception, she had Ventus at her side as a constant companion and friend.

Aquata kept her eyes on the sea. "I don't. I can't make heads or tails of it. Ventus and I talked long into the night. Neither of us could decide what it means. Why can't you put this behind you? Your work is more important than this momentary sensation."

Fauna had hoped to find some compassion from her sister, but being made of water, Aquata had little to give. She tugged her shawl more snugly around her shoulders and found small comfort in it. "This experience has left me changed. It's opened a new place in my heart and left it raw and aching. Whatever happiness I thought I had in the past is nothing more than a shadow of what it could have been. Of what my heart is capable of feeling."

"There is satisfaction in your work, a sense of pride, isn't there? Who's to say that you won't feel this greater happiness doing it, now that you know about it?"

"Because it's not the same!" Fauna shouted. Her face grew hot, and her pulse quickened. Aquata leaned away from her, surprised at the sudden outburst. Ventus, who had been listening nearby, startled and for a moment reverted into a gust of wind.

She relaxed her hands, which had balled into fists, and let them fall into her lap, ashamed at losing her composure. "I'm no longer content. I have seen something greater, something more beautiful in the world, and I want to have a part in it.

It's as if I've been in the dark, blindly doing what I always have done, and yesterday, I was shown the light. It has meaning. I need to figure out what that is."

"You've decided then," Ventus said. "You wish to travel to Terran's mount and speak with him."

Fauna shifted her gaze from the advancing and retreating tide and looked toward her older brother. "If he knows anything about this, anything, then he might be able to help me. This longing, it's unbearable. The more I try to ignore it, the greater it grows. I can't bear to think that I am fated to spend all of eternity alone."

"Then you must go. Will you allow Ventus and me to travel with you?" Aquata asked, turning her crystalline blue eyes on Fauna.

Normally, she would welcome the chance to spend the long hours of walking with her siblings, but the thought of conversation, especially when it would be focused around her, made her uneasy. "You have your own work to do. The winds and the waves need you."

"The mountain streams and breezes need us as well. When will we go?" Aquata wouldn't be deterred so easily.

Fauna ran a hand through her hair, unsure of how to tell them that she would rather not have them along. "I know you feel like you must protect me, and I appreciate it, really. But for now, I need some time to myself. I will be traveling alone."

Ventus opened his mouth to protest but was silenced by Aquata's upheld hand. "It's a long way. Are you certain you don't want our company?"

"Yes, the walk will give me the chance to think of ways this problem can be solved." She stood and brushed the sand from her draping robe and pulled it tighter around her body. "I'll leave after the sun passes its peak."

The afternoon came with the smell of the sea mixed with the dust of the dry grasses. From her tower door, the mountain where Terran made his home loomed off to the east. Fauna stepped out the door and a cool breeze laden with mist swirled around her.

The twin voices of her brother and sister floated up from the gathering mist. "You're certain about this? You still feel you need to make this journey?"

"I don't have a choice. Terran possesses greater knowledge than all of us. He keeps the records of the eternities. If anyone is able to help, it's him."

Aquata's face formed in the mist. "Go then. The sooner you find what you seek, the sooner you can be happy again."

Fauna felt a pang as she watched them swirl away, but she knew it was for the best. Having them around would have made it impossible to figure out what she was going to tell Terran. If she couldn't convince him about how she needed this emotion for herself, he might dismiss her feelings as foolishness and insist that she return to her work and forget the whole incident.

Tall grasses bowed along either side of the narrow trail that led to the mount. Fauna let their feathered heads tickle her palms as she passed. Further up the trail, a chorus of chitters rang out from a copse of twisted oak trees as a family of squirrels raced from branch to branch, scolding and chasing one another.

As she passed, she reached out a mental thread to a silver-tailed squirrel working the cap off of an acorn. She was not surprised to find his thoughts centering entirely on the prize he held. She carefully pushed the thread deeper. She had to know if this squirrel felt the mysterious emotion as well. Hidden beneath all the superficial thoughts of food, she found what she sought, a deep longing that rivaled her own.

Seconds later, a bushy brown she-squirrel ran up to the silver-tailed squirrel's branch and chased him down into the brush. In that moment, his longing switched to joy and confirmed what Fauna had suspected from the beginning: Apollo wasn't the only one capable of feeling this aching longing.

Again and again, she reached out to her different creations as she made her way towards the mount, from the mighty wild horses of the grassy plains to the dormant bats that hung in the hollows of fallen trees, and each time, she found this deeper, richer sense of belonging.

Between the long flats of the grassland and the beginning of the rolling hills leading to the mountain, Fauna realized that she was no longer alone. Trailing along behind her and off to the side of the trail, she caught sight of a playful mist darting behind trees and low bushes whenever she turned. The thought of Ventus and Aquata coming to check on her should have bothered her, as she had asked them to leave her alone. Instead, catching them trying to hide from her only made her smile. She would rather have them care too much for her than too little. They followed for a short while before rushing off once more.

Fauna reached the foot of Terran's mount as the sun touched the horizon. The ocean shimmered in the distance and led her eye to the familiar rise in the cliff and her tower. It had only been a day since her discovery, and yet the whole world had changed. She had changed. This new awareness within her had opened her eyes and heart, and what used to be familiar was now new again.

At the foot of the trail, Fauna heard the familiar rumbling of her eldest brother's voice echoing from above, and she wondered to whom he was speaking.

The path leading to Terran's cave wound back and forth up the steep mountainside. At each turn, the voices became clearer and more distinct from each other. Her stomach sank. She had hoped to have this time with Terran to herself. Instead, she found all of her brothers and sisters, including Aquata and Ventus, seated in the wide mouth of his cave.

Terran's massive bulk rested on the boulder that he had crafted into a seat, making it hard to tell where the seat ended and his body began. He leaned forward to listen to Flora, who perched in her narrow seat, her vine and branch arms crossed over the bark of her legs. A yellow rose blossomed above her ear. The twins huddled in their corner of the cave, locked in what looked like a serious conversation. All four were so intent in their discussions that no one noticed Fauna when she entered the cave's mouth. She cleared her throat, effectively silencing them all.

Ventus darted toward her, with Aquata trailing close behind. "Please, don't be angry. We told him you were coming, that's all."

"I told you I wanted to speak with Terran alone." Fauna dug her nails into her palms and tried to rein in her anger at the twins. "What is the meaning of this?"

Before they could explain, Terran approached her with arms outstretched. "It's not their fault. I asked them to be here. It's good to see you after so long, Fauna."

She welcomed his embrace. In his arms, the emptiness inside seemed not as vast. Had the other siblings not been watching, she would have spent hours there, letting the hurt drain away. "It's good to be here."

Terran looked down at her with his deep amethyst eyes. "The twins have told me what they could of what has been bothering you. I would like to hear it from you so I can be sure I understand." Terran dried her eyes with his thumb. His voice echoed within him like a cavern. "My, my, this is serious. I have never seen you so."

She sighed, and Terran released her from his arms. "I've discovered something, and it's shaken me deeply. I don't know what it is. I was hoping that you might know." She looked into his angular face. He, like her other siblings, did not have a heart of flesh. His was one of clay, rugged and slow to change. She prayed that somewhere in his infinite wisdom, he would know what she needed. "I was hoping to share this with you alone." She shot a look at Ventus and Aquata. It would be a while before she could trust them again.

Terran led her to her seat in the circle. "Both Flora and I would like to hear about what is troubling you. Please, tell us what happened."

Fauna glanced around the circle, still uncomfortable to be speaking in front of all four of her siblings. She cleared her throat and wove her fingers in front of her, unsure of where to start.

"Yesterday, I learned that I was alone in the world. All the creations I tend to will one day find a mate, someone of their kind that they can spend their lives with. Until yesterday, it was simply part of the cycle and a required part of ensuring the growth of the species.

"Then there was Apollo, the albatross I raised from a chick. We became close over the years, and it seemed natural to be with him when it came time for him to court his own mate. It was then I realized there was something much more important going on between these creatures than mating. They care for each other, they crave each other, and there is a longing that only being together can relieve. This longing runs deeper than anything I've ever experienced. I can't believe that I've lived this long and never felt its like before.

"Being a witness to Apollo's courtship opened something within me, a vast emptiness that I cannot fill. Now I long for something I can share my life with, someone I can care for, someone that will care for me as well."

Terran cupped his chin in his hand. "I believe I know of what you speak, but I must be sure," he said, regarding her thoughtfully. "The dirt of the field longs for water when the rains are long in coming. The volcano longs for release when the pressure builds. Is this the same?"

"That's what I want to know as well," Flora added. "A flower's purpose is to attract the bee to be pollinated so that a seed may form. Shouldn't fulfilling your duties fill this need within you?"

"No, it's not the same," Fauna answered. "Once the earth is moist, it no longer thinks of rain. Once the volcano has erupted, it is satisfied until the pressure builds again. When my creations select a mate, the longing does not end. They long for their mate regardless of the circumstance. It is as if they each hold a piece of the other's heart. Only together can they live."

"And you? Does something hold a piece of your heart?" Terran asked, his words tender and low.

"How, dear brother?" Fauna asked, her voice breaking. "There are none like me with whom I can share it. All the creatures of the earth have those like them for companionship. I have none. Even among ourselves, we are so very different from each other."

Terran let out a long, slow breath and exchanged a look with Flora. "We knew this day would come. One day, you would be shown the deeper and greater power that exists between the creatures of field and sea. I know this longing that you speak of. It has a name."

That caught Fauna's attention, she sat straighter. "What then, what is it?"

"Love."

The sound of the word rang true in Fauna's ears and felt familiar, as if she had been told about it a long time ago, long before memory, almost like a dream. It echoed through the empty space within her, and she knew it was what she had felt and what she now craved. "Why would you keep this knowledge from me?"

Terran stood and turned toward the wall, unable to face her. "Because love is the one thing that Guardians cannot have. You, as a creature of the flesh, would feel its absence the most keenly of us all, so we chose to keep you innocent of its existence. We knew that it couldn't last forever, and we are grateful that so many years passed where you could live peacefully and do your work. I'm afraid that now you know of it, you will never truly be at peace again."

"I don't want to live like this. There has to be a way. Please tell me that there is a way," she begged.

"It is as you said before. There is no one like you here in this world. The love that you crave can only exist between two creatures who are the same. I'm sorry." Terran's shoulders slumped forward, and he sought Flora's hand for comfort.

The finality of Terran's words fell like a great weight, crushing Fauna's already fragile spirit. She couldn't breathe. She could no longer live. When she tried to speak, the only word her mouth would make was "no." She heard herself repeat it over and over until she was screaming.

For an untold amount of time, she lost hold of reality and slipped into a place where there was neither sound nor sensation. Her own cries sounded far away, like they belonged to someone else. A pair of strong arms wrapped around her and rocked her like a child.

Reality crept back, raw and harsh, and she heard a voice calling her name. She blinked. Terran had cradled her against his chest, trying to comfort her. Flora stood nearby along with the twins, concern painted over their features as they helplessly watched on.

"Easy there, you're all right... Just breathe," Terran said as he stroked her hair.

The world seemed to spin around her. If it wasn't for Terran's anchoring presence, she felt as if she might be flung away. "I'm so lost, Terran. I don't know what to do."

He cleared his throat. "Return to your tower. Restore order among your creations. You may find joy in their joy. They still need your guidance and are comforted in your presence. Dwelling on this will only bring more pain."

"You and I both know that it won't work. There has to be something else. I'd rather die than live without hope." She brushed the hair away from her face and found it wet with tears.

Terran set Fauna down into her seat. "Please don't talk like that."

Anger and desperation crept up from deep within Fauna's chest, making it hard to not shout. She gripped the edge of her robe, pressing her nails into the cloth as hard as she could. "Why not? I now know that I will never find joy or peace in my life again. What reason do I have to live for?"

Terran settled back into his own massive seat with a groan and ran a hand over his stony head. "You have your duty as a Guardian. Your creations still need you. There are creations that you haven't imagined yet that need to be made."

"No. My creations can care for themselves. That is the way I created them. They don't need me for guidance any longer." She loosened her grip to place a hand over her aching heart. "As for new creations, how do you expect me to imagine anything other than my own pain?"

Terran lifted his face, revealing a great sorrow creasing his hard features. "There is something—"

Flora flowed to her feet and halted him with a twiggy hand. "It's forbidden. You must not speak of it."

Terran pushed the hand away and shifted to face her. "I cannot stand by and watch her suffer, and neither can you. We knew from the beginning that this day would come, and now it's here." He sighed and lowered his voice. "The instructions in the scrolls are clear. We have no choice but to ease her heart and bring her the love that she so desperately seeks. Will you aid me or not?"

Flora glanced from Fauna back to Terran. Her stiff wooden features softened from absolution to agreement. "You know what this will cost us, Terran. I don't like it. I wish there was some other way."

He placed his massive hand on her shoulder, being careful not to snap her branches. "You know this is the only way. This is how it was meant to be."

Flora nodded and turned away, hugging her arms around herself as if warding off a chill.

Fauna pushed her way between them. "What way? What are you talking about?"

"You will learn of it soon enough. I must be sure that it will work. It has only been done once before," Terran said. "For now, I need you to return to your tower and do your best to fulfill your responsibilities. Watch for me, I will come to you when all is prepared."

Ventus and Aquata had grown restless and swayed and spun in slow ripples across the wide opening of the cave mouth as they listened.

"Come, sister," they pleaded, "come away now." Ventus tugged at the edge of her sleeve.

Before turning to leave, Fauna reached out to her elder brother. He took her extended hand in his own massive hand. She could not help but notice the change in him. His easy smile seemed forced now, his movements slow and deliberate.

"Something is troubling you." She spoke so that only he could hear. "What's this about a cost?"

"Do you trust me?" His quietest voice still made the air around her tremble.

"Always. You know that."

He squeezed her hand gently. "Then I must ask you to continue to do so. This is an event that has been a thousand years in the making. Your discovery means change, and change can be difficult to accept. I will make this right, if I can."

Terran turned away, leaving Fauna to be guided from the cave by Ventus. There was so much more she wanted to ask her eldest brother, so much she still didn't understand.

Sketches of half of a lacy wing, the bones of a bird's skull, the dorsal fin of a fish, and other half-imagined creatures sprawled over dozens of papers that lay scattered over Fauna's worktable and across the floor, each one incomplete, flawed, and broken. Her love and respect for Terran had been enough to push her to keep trying, at least for a while, but the strain was wearing her down.

Days turned to weeks, and the emerald green of the distant oak trees burned crimson with the changing of the seasons. The ink well on the table had long since dried up, along with the strength and focus required to create life. Evening communion became too painful to perform. Each morning, her struggle to rise became more difficult. Each evening, she returned to her bed sooner.

One morning, the wind stopped. The endless crashing of waves subsided. Even buried deep in her despair, the silence jarred her senses. An eerie calm remained unbroken for the space of a day. Fauna left her bed and sat at the window, wondering where Aquata and Ventus had gone. A familiar cry drew her attention skyward, and she spotted Apollo wheeling in the sky nearby with his mate.

As the birds passed from view, Fauna felt her tower shift and tremble. It could only mean one thing: Terran approached. The thought lightened her heart, and she raced down the twisted tower steps and out the heavy door. At the rise in the hill, he approached in long, slow strides, each step making the earth thunder.

She waited there on the rise, pacing and fretting. The stillness of the air hung heavily around her. Terran held something tiny in his massive arms. When he reached the top of the hill, he knelt before Fauna. His movements spoke of great fatigue as if he had struggled for a long time. He leaned forward to show her what he held. "This is a child, an infant for you to raise as your own. I searched through all the ancient scrolls, through the very blueprints of the world, until I found the answer." He stroked the child's cheek with an unexpected gentleness. "When the Guardians were created, they came forth one at a time. I came first, to guard the fledgling earth. Then wind and water came to prepare the way for life. Flora was next, bringing growing things. When all was prepared, the Fates created you."

Fauna furrowed her brow. "This child is formed from clay and vine. How do you expect me to love him as my own?"

"He is not yet complete. Your brother and sisters have worked tirelessly with me to create him. Now, only one step remains. Your powers are needed to transform him from clay into flesh. He needs a soul."

Terran set the clay child down before her in a nest of grass. His delicate features were sculpted from the same dark clay from which her brother was made. Woven just beneath the child's skin were vines and roots mimicking the fine vessels that spider-webbed underneath her own.

The breeze curled around them, bringing with it a fine mist. Aquata and Ventus appeared.

"We all took part in the child's creation," said Aquata.

Ventus nodded in agreement.

Fauna reached her hand toward the clay child, unsure whether she should touch him or not. She looked up toward her siblings. "I thought Flora was against this."

"All the siblings worked together, adding their skill and elements of themselves. Once Flora was convinced of the wisdom in this, she agreed. She cares as much as the rest of us." He placed a huge hand over the clay child's chest, taking care not to crush him. "He is a complete creation. If you grant him a soul, he will live."

Fauna pulled her arms tight around herself. Terran had brought her a child that she could raise as her own. How could she accept such great a gift? In her heart, she knew this to be the answer, but a helplessness held her in its grip just as loneliness had before. A child, to love, rear, and teach, waited for her touch. Tending to all the creations in the world had not prepared her to be a mother. The weight of responsibility hung heavy in the air.

"Will you accept the child?" Aquata asked.

Both she and Ventus stood, still and quiet, unusual for them, waiting for her answer.

"I am not sure. I do not quite know what it will mean if I do."

Terran turned so he faced her, his immense back to the others. "Do not decide right away; give yourself time. I will return in a fortnight and reclaim him if need be."

Fauna nodded. She was so full of conflicting emotion that she feared if she opened her mouth, a tumble of feelings would come streaming out over the ground.

Terran spoke to the other siblings before they left her with the child. Alone, she sank to her knees next to the tiny, lifeless body. Hours passed as she sat by his side, motionless, lost in thought. The bright light of day faded, replaced by the more subtle light of the moon.

Night came and went, and the world held its breath.

With the coming of the dawn came new awareness. Stirrings of love, so thrilling and complete, washed over her as she gazed at the child. She knew he had to be hers. There, in the cool morning light, she touched him for the first time, brushing her fingertips across his brow, the feather-soft grass of his hair tickling her fingers.

For the remainder of the second day and into the third, Fauna weighed out the elements of her soul she wished the child to have. He would need both kindness and strength in his heart and wisdom and justice in his thoughts. Everything she valued, she wished for him to have.

On the morning of the fourth day, the sun rose, casting its warming rays across the land. As the light touched the child, Fauna took him into her arms and granted him exactly half of her soul. As her half left her body and entered his, she watched in wonder as the greys and browns of his earthy body faded into the pink of rose-petal soft skin. His wispy, grassy hair changed from pale green to a deep brown.

He was perfect. Every eyelash, every toe, even the tiny curve inside his ear was perfect. But he was still; he had not stirred or taken a breath. Anxious moments passed and she wondered if she had done something wrong.

There was only one thing to do, and it frightened her what it might mean should she attempt it. She weighed out another measure of her soul, enough to tip the balance between them, and held it between her fingers. A sacrifice such as this would have its price. Would whatever she lost be worth the joy and fulfillment she would gain by raising a son? When thinking of the emptiness of her earlier existence, she couldn't bear to return to how things used to be.

With great care, she released that last measure into his tiny body. His eyelids fluttered, and he took a first deep breath before releasing a cry that filled her with immeasurable joy. He was hers. She was his. They would complete each other. She held him close to her chest, wrapped her shawl around him, and rocked him until he calmed.

Apollo flew close overhead, extending a wing toward her. She reached out to him, as she had done so many times before, this time to share the tidings of her son. After all, he had been the catalyst for all of this to come about, and she wanted to thank him. To her dismay, she found she could not form the channel between them, she could not share her feelings with him. It was as if he wasn't there. He landed nearby and walked up to her, his head cocked to one side as if questioning what was wrong.

"Apollo, come. It's all right. I'm still the same as before. It's just . . ." She reached out a hand to stroke his feathers, and he shied away. "I promise I'm still your friend. Please believe me."

The great bird hopped further away and shrieked at them before beating his wings and taking to the sky. The noise startled the baby, and he began to whimper.

"No, Apollo, no! This isn't right. I won't harm you. Please trust me." Her pleas did not reach him and he flew away, back to the cliffs, back to his mate. She cuddled the infant closer, resting his head in the curve of her neck. She breathed in his scent and let his presence fill her. The loss of Apollo's friendship cut deeply, and she would miss him. This must have been what Terran meant when he spoke of a cost.

She was no longer a Guardian.

Her attention returned to the baby, now curled up against her chest. She already loved him more fiercely than she could ever imagine. He needed her and she needed him. The pain of her loneliness had been transformed into something new and wonderful. Having her awareness opened to feel love had brought her anguish, but through it, she would now be able to taste the heights of happiness.

A playful breeze tossed at her clothes and gusted around her in circles. Ventus, along with her other siblings, had not ventured far during her time of reflection. She strained her eyes, seeking his familiar face in the wind.

"Brother?" she called.

There was no reply; the silence made her stomach turn. She pulled the shawl closer around her and the baby. Ventus should have been right there. She could have sworn she had felt his touch.

A mist flowed up from the sea and Fauna stood, eager to show Aquata her child. She waited to see her sister's face, but none formed in the mist.

"Sister?"

Again, no answer.

The realization hit with such force that the pain of it drove her to her knees. If she was no longer a Guardian, she could no longer be with her beloved siblings. Ventus would no longer sit on her windowsill to talk. Aquata would no longer give her advice. Flora would no longer be her unwavering voice of reason. She wouldn't be able to run to Terran's arms for comfort. And that hurt most of all.

The child stirred and opened his eyes, as blue and deep as the ocean, and in them, she saw Aquata. As he breathed, she felt the air move and in it, found Ventus. He clenched his fist around her finger. He would be strong like noble Terran. In the curls of his chestnut brown hair, she saw Flora. In every part of her precious child, she saw each of her siblings. She knew she would never be alone.

The wind felt harsher and coarser against her skin, and dark clouds began to loom overhead. In the distance, a flash of lightning split the sky and the ground trembled. She carried her precious child back to the tower, up to the safety of the turret. Terran had spoken about change, about how it was necessary even if it would cause pain. The reality of those words became clear as the storm began to rage unlike any she had seen before. Her siblings had each sacrificed part of their Guardianship in order to create the child and their hold on the world had weakened.

Wind poured in through the open window and filled her ears with a wild rush and at the edge, a sound, a question. They were there, they had to be.

She went to the window and cried out to the sky, "I will call him Adam!"

Also by Jodi L. Milner

The Shadow Barrier Trilogy: A Young Adult Coming of Age Epic Fantasy Series

Stonebearer's Betrayal

Stonebearer's Apprentice

Stonebearer's Redemption

Join Jodi L. Milner's Reading Community

If you enjoyed this story, be sure to sign up for Jodi's mailing list and be the first to score free stories, new release info, updates, and enter to win contests.

Go here: https://subscribepage.io/jodilmilner

Or scan here:

About the Author

Jodi L. Milner is the author of The Shadow Barrier Trilogy, a YA coming of age fantasy series, which has won several awards including the prestigious Diamond Quill from the League of Utah Writers in 2023. She's also a cohost of Squirrel! The Podcast for the Distracted Writer, runs a small virtual assisting business helping author clients overcome their technical challenges, and teaches at local writing conferences.

When not chasing daydreams or her children, she enjoys destroying movie plots, making amigurumi, and plotting to take over the world.

Find out more at JodiLMilner.com